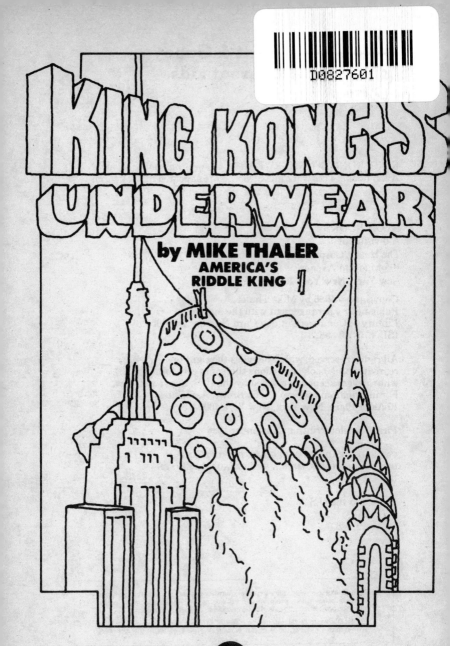

KING KONG'S UNDERWEAR

by MIKE THALER
AMERICA'S RIDDLE KING

AN AVON CAMELOT BOOK

For Matt & Gabby
two great kids

KING KONG'S UNDERWEAR is an original publication of Avon Books. This work has never before appeared in book form.

AVON BOOKS
A division of
The Hearst Corporation
105 Madison Avenue
New York, New York 10016

First Camelot Printing: November 1986

CAMELOT TRADEMARK REG. U.S. PAT. OFF. AND IN
OTHER COUNTRIES, MARCA REGISTRADA, HECHO EN
U.S.A.

Printed in the U.S.A.

OPM 10 9 8 7

DETECTIVE STORY

I'M A GUMSHOE

A PRIVATE EYE

I PACK A BIG HEATER

ONE DAY I WAS COMBING THE CITY

WHEN I SPOTTED A CROOK

I TAILED 'IM

HE JUMPED BAIL

6

THE POLICE GRILLED 'IM

BOOKED 'IM

AND PUT 'IM IN THE PEN.

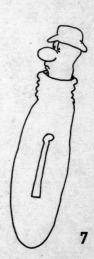

7

FUNNY NOSES

PIANOSE

VOLCANOSE

RHINOSE

**THE WIZARD
OF SNOZ**

U.F. NOSE

MINNOSE

TICKLETOONS

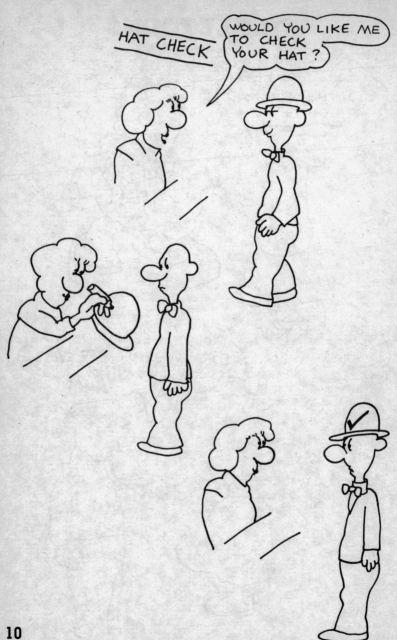

THE SMARTEST DOG
IN THE WORLD

14

FUNNY MOONS

MOON LIGHT

NAPOLEON MOONAPART

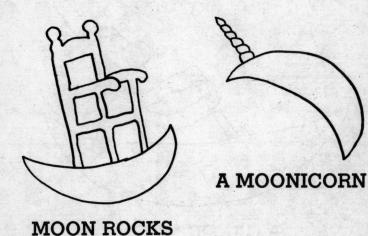

A MOONICORN

MOON ROCKS

A HONEYMOON

A MOON ON
THE WANE

A CANOE MOON

WHAT KIND OF
LIGHTS ARE THESE?

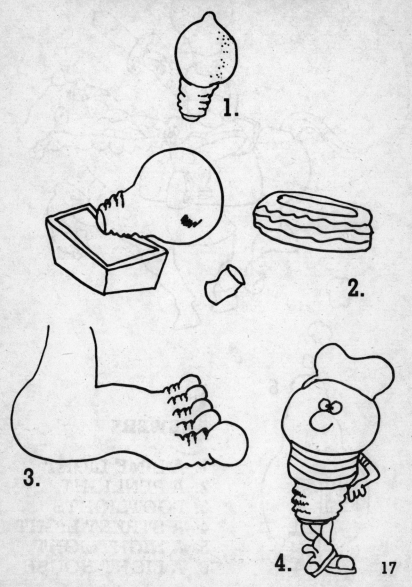

1.

2.

3.

4.

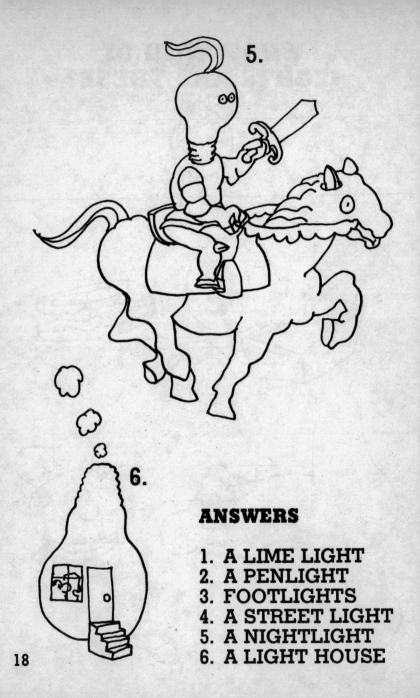

5.

6.

ANSWERS

1. A LIME LIGHT
2. A PENLIGHT
3. FOOTLIGHTS
4. A STREET LIGHT
5. A NIGHTLIGHT
6. A LIGHT HOUSE

LIGHT HUMOR

THE POLE VOLT

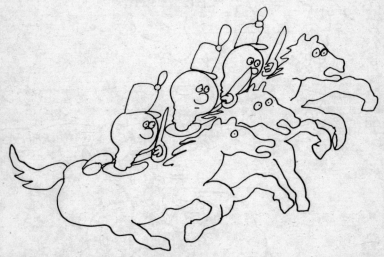

THE CHARGE OF THE LIGHT BRIGADE

A FLASH FLOOD

WHIZDUMB

MAN WHO CUTS WAY
THROUGH JUNGLE
GETS BUSHED

MAN WHO CALL HAWAII
GET SARONG NUMBER

MAN WHO EATS 10,000 BANANAS HAS LOTS OF APPEAL

IF YOU DRIVE A CAR FOR SOMEONE ELSE YOU'VE GOT NOTHING TO CHAUFFEUR IT

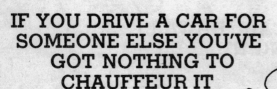

PROGRESS I

**EARLY RACE CARS
LOOKED LIKE THIS**

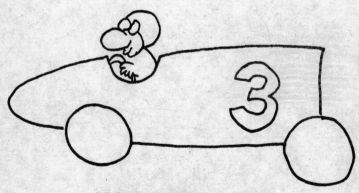

**NOW RACE CARS
LOOK LIKE THIS**

WHAT FAMOUS LIGHT STARRED IN "SATURDAY LIGHT FEVER"?

JOHN TRAVOLTA

WHAT LIGHT WAS A FAMOUS ARCHITECT?

FRANK LLOYD LIGHT

WHAT TWO LIGHTS WERE FAMOUS PHILOSOPHERS?

SOCKETES AND VOLTAIRE

WHAT LIGHT WAS A FAMOUS BOXER?

NEON SPINKS

WHAT LIGHT WAS A FAMOUS GANGSTER?

BULBY FACE NELSON

THE OLD WEST

COW GOSSIP

PIGS AT HOME

FUNNY SNAKES

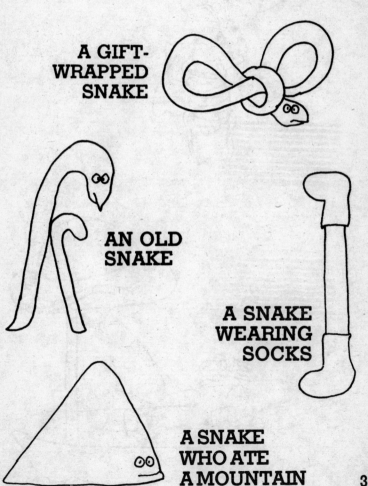

A SNAKE
WITH HICCUPS

A GIFT-
WRAPPED
SNAKE

AN OLD
SNAKE

A SNAKE
WEARING
SOCKS

A SNAKE
WHO ATE
A MOUNTAIN

WHAT IS IT?

1.

2.

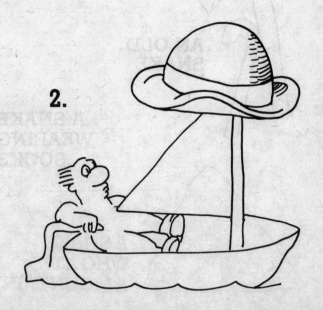

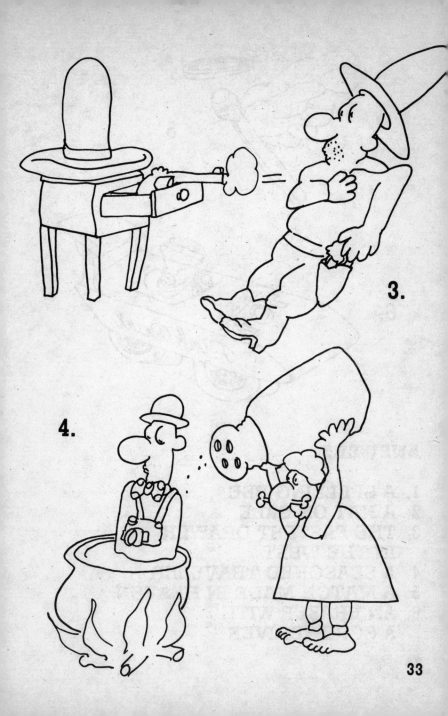

3.

4.

33

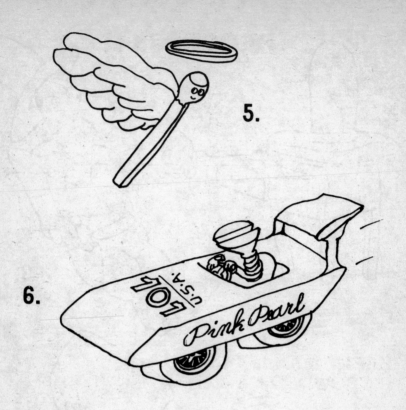

5.

6.

ANSWERS

1. A SPELLING BEE
2. A HAT ON SALE
3. THE FASTEST DRAWER
   IN THE WEST
4. A SEASONED TRAVELER
5. A MATCH MADE IN HEAVEN
6. AN ERASER WITH
   A SCREWDRIVER

PROGRESS II

EARLY MAN LIVED IN
CROWDED CAVES

BUT TODAY...

THE SMARTEST BIRD
IN THE WORLD

37

FUNNY LIGHTS

SHEDDING LIGHT

LIGHT AS A FEATHER

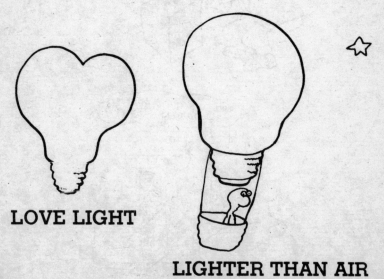

LOVE LIGHT

LIGHTER THAN AIR

A BRIGHT IDEA

LIGHT HUMOR

THE SPEED OF LIGHT

HOW FAST DOES LIGHT REALLY TRAVEL?

IN A RACE CAR VERY FAST

JOGGING ... NOT SO FAST

ABROAD VERY SLOW

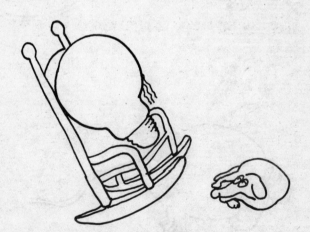

**AND WHEN THEY GET OLD
THEY HARDLY LEAVE
HOME AT ALL**

A SNOUTLET

WHERE DO THEY GET GAS?

A TURTLE?

AT A SHELL STATION

A CHICKEN?

AT AN EGGSON STATION

A PIG?

AT HAMOCO

A COW?

AT MOOBIL

A BELLY BUTTON?

AT A BP STATION

AND WINTER?

AT SNOWCO

PICTURE POEMS

AN ELEPHANT PIZZA

A BAD SCOOP OF ICE CREAM

A BUTTERFLY
PENCIL

A HINDU SPOON CHARMER

A PIPE DREAM

46

PROGRESS III

**EARLY MAN USED TO
DRAW ON WALLS**

BUT TODAY...

TALKING THINGS

EDIBLE ANIMALS

A STRAWBERRY RABBIT

A HIP-POTATO-MUS

A BANANOCTOPUS

A PICKLE FROG

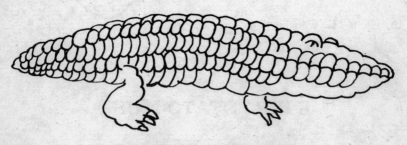

A CROCORNDILE

SMALL TALK

52

MORE TICKLETOONS

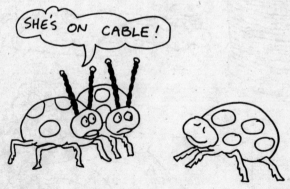

54

A LIGHT BULB
TURNING INTO A PIG

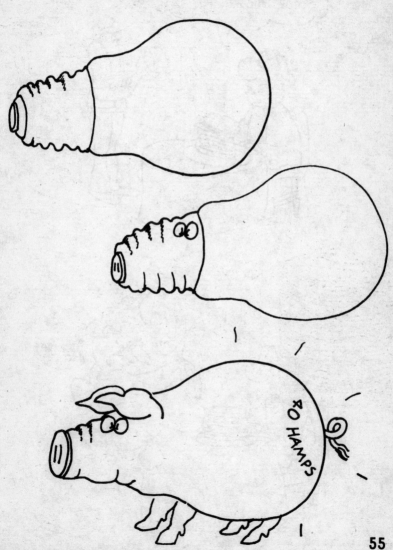

CREATIVE WAITER I

CREATIVE WAITER II

CREATIVE WAITER III

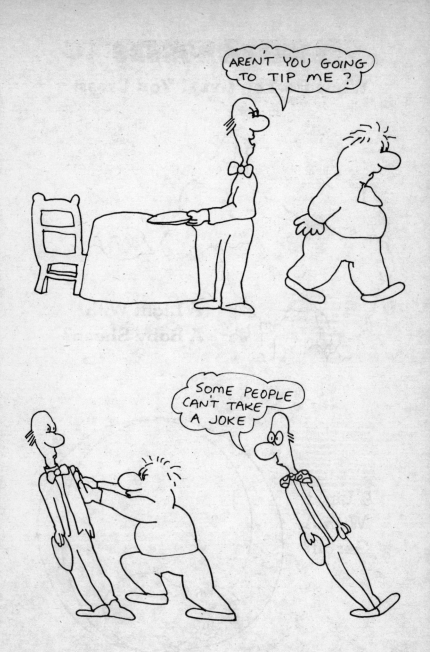

59

LIGHT CROSSES
What Do You Get If You Cross:

1.

A Light With
A Baby Sheep?

A Light
With A
Gerbil?

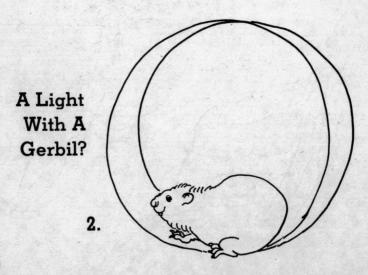

2.

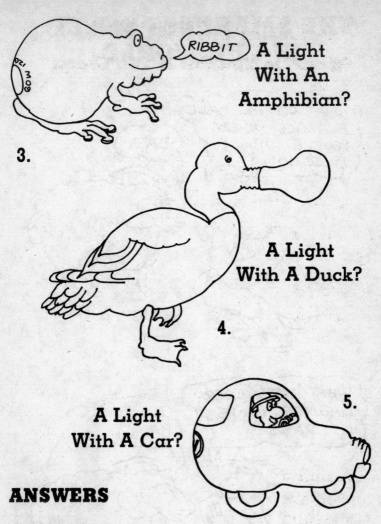

**A Light
With An
Amphibian?**

3.

**A Light
With A Duck?**

4.

**A Light
With A Car?**

5.

ANSWERS

1. LAMP
2. AN AMSTER
3. A BULB FROG
4. AN ELECTRIC BILL
5. A VOLTSWAGON

THE SMARTEST SHEEP
IN THE WORLD

PROGRESS IV

PRIMITIVE MAN USED TO LEAVE
HIS MESS AROUND HIM

BUT TODAY...

MORE WHAT IS IT?

1.

2.

3.

4.

5.

6.

ANSWERS

1. A MATERIAL WITNESS
2. A MAN SERVING TIME
3. A STEP CHILD
4. A LADY WITH A MOLE
   ON HER NOSE
5. A HIT RECORD
6. A SLEEPING BAG

HAMINALS

What Do You Get If You Cross A Pig With A:

LION?

A SWION

With An Owl?

A SOWL

With A Crocodile?

A HOCKADILE

With A Flamingo?

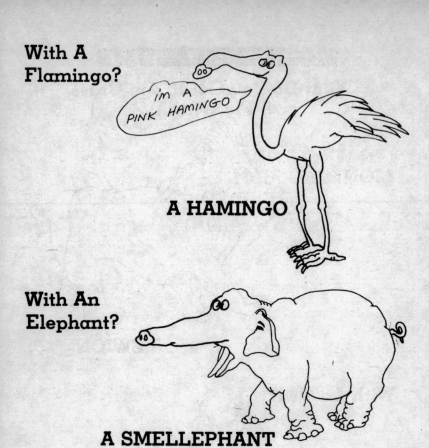

A HAMINGO

With An Elephant?

A SMELLEPHANT

And With A Snake?

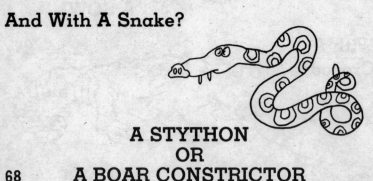

A STYTHON
OR
A BOAR CONSTRICTOR

MORE WHIZDUMB

MAN WHO SWIMS IN
APPLE JUICE IS
INSIDER

MAN WHO TRIES
TO MAKE
INDIAN DRESS IS
SEW SARI

**MAN WHO GOES
CAMPING
IS INTENSE**

**MAN WHO JUMPS
INTO BLENDER
IS ALL MIXED UP**

A LIGHT BIT

WHERE ARE YOU FROM?

LOVE TALK OR
A HOT ROMANCE

MORE FUNNY NOSES

THE NOSE BOWL

CYRANOSE

PETE NOSE

THE COSA
NOSE·TRA

HYPNOSES

FUNNY FISHES

AN OVER ACHIEVER

SUSPICIOUS FISHES

A CLAM WEARING A WALKMAN

A FISH CRYING

AN OCEAN-GOING TUNA

A FISH IN LOVE

EVEN MORE TICKLETOONS

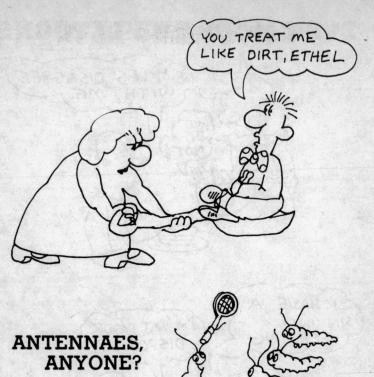

ANTENNAES, ANYONE?

78

SOMETHING ELSE

AN ALLIWAITER

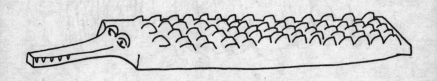

A CROCOFILE

MICE CREAM

AN ANTHEATER

A GIRAFT

A LLAMA-HA

LIGHT CONVERSATION

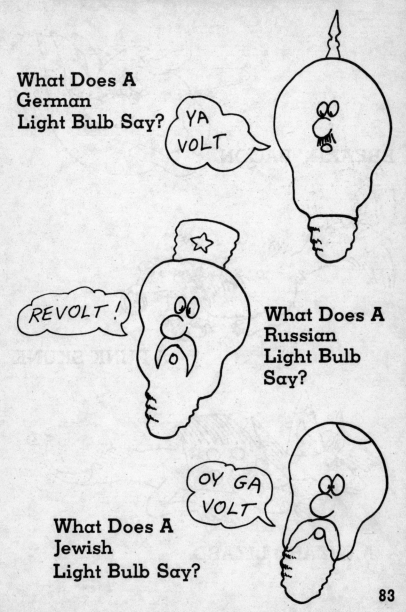

SOME OTHER THINGS

BREAKIN' BACON

A PUNK SKUNK

A WIZARD LIZARD

84

A VERY HIP-POPOTAMUS

EVEN MORE WHAT IS IT?

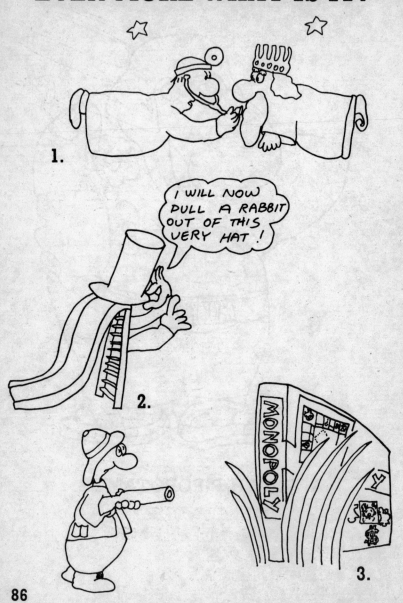

ANSWERS

1. DOC-KING IN SPACE
2. A SLIDE SHOW
3. A BIG GAME HUNTER
4. A LADY WEARING PUMPS
5. A BREAKDANCER
6. A MAN RUNNING AT
   A FAST CLIP

AND MORE PICTURE POEMS

THE OCTOPUS STRING QUARTET

A WALRUS PIE

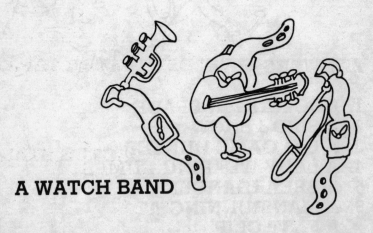

A WATCH BAND

A FROG AT A PARTY

A WILD RADIATOR TAMER

CACTUS STARS

MEDICAL TALK

BOAT TALK

HOW EDISON INVENTED
THE LIGHT BULB

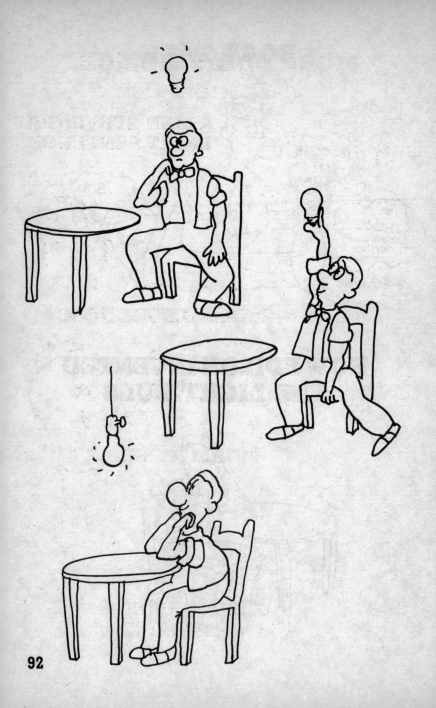

MORE LIGHT HUMOR

A MAN SERVING A LIGHT SENTENCE

A MAN WITH A BULBOUS NOSE

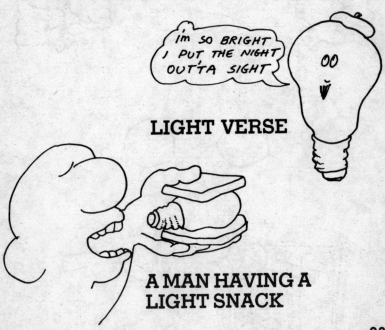

LIGHT VERSE

A MAN HAVING A LIGHT SNACK

PROGRESS V

PRIMITIVE MAN USED
TO THROW ROCKS WHEN
HE WENT TO WAR

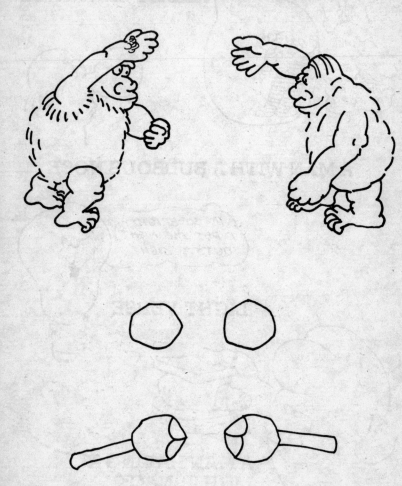

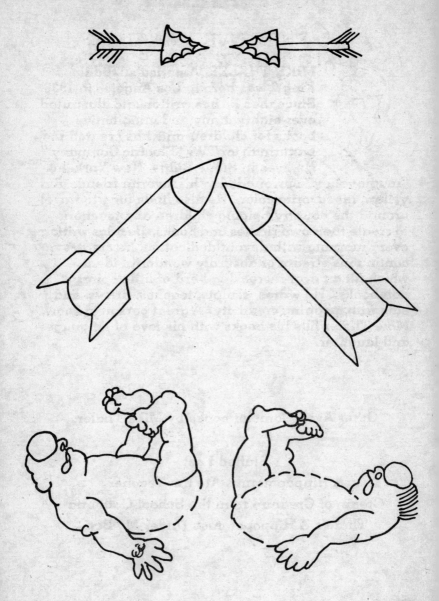

MIKE THALER, America's "Riddle King," was born in Los Angeles in 1936. Since then he has written and illustrated over eighty funny and imaginative books for children and has created the Letterman for TV's "Electric Company." He lives in Stone Ridge, New York, his "magic valley," surrounded by his favorite friends and yellow, his favorite color. He also finds time to travel around the country helping children and teachers to create their own riddles and books. Besides writing every morning with devout dedication, he creates a continuous stream of absurdly wonderful ideas, which fill an ever-increasing herd of little spiral notebooks. He writes, sculpts, teaches, draws, and eats with inspiring creativity. A great person to know, Mike Thaler fills his books with his love of language and laughter.

Other Avon Camelot books by Mike Thaler:

Stuffed Feet
A Hippopotamus Ate the Teacher
Cream of Creature from the School Cafeteria
There's A Hippopotamus Under My Bed